PICTURE BOOK STUDIO USA

Copyright, © 1982, Verlag Neugebauer Press, Salzburg, Austria.
Original title: NUSSKNACKER UND MAUSEKÖNIG
Text copyright, © 1983, Neugebauer Press USA, Inc.
PICTURE BOOK STUDIO is an imprint of Neugebauer Press USA, Inc.
Distributed by Alphabet Press, Natick, MA

All Rights Reserved.
Printed in Austria by Druckhaus Nonntal, Salzburg.
ISBN 0-907234-33-X

Library of Congress Cataloging in Publication Data
Hoffmann, E.T.A. (Ernst Theodor Amadeus), 1776-1822
The Nutcracker.
Original title: Nussknacker und Mausekönig.
Summary: After hearing how her toy nutcracker got
his ugly face, a little girl helps break the spell and
changes him into a handsome prince.
[1. Fairy tales] I. Zwerger, Lisbeth, ill.
II. Bell, Anthea. III. Title.
PZ8.S31276Nu 1983 [Fic] 83-8092
ISBN 0-907234-33-X

E.T.A.Hoffmann

THE NUTCRACKER
AND THE MOUSE-KING

illustrated by Lisbeth Zwerger
translated and adapted by Anthea Bell

CHRISTMAS EVE

On Christmas Eve, the Stahlbaum children were not allowed in the living room all day, let alone the grand drawing room next to it. It was evening now, and twilight, and there were no lamps lit in the little back room where Fritz and Marie were sitting.

Fritz was whispering to his little sister, who was only just seven, telling her about the rustling, bumping, thudding noises he had heard going on behind the locked doors all day. Not so long ago, said Fritz, he'd seen a little man hurrying across the hall with a big box tucked under his arm, and he knew that was Godfather Drosselmeier.

"Oh, I wonder what he's made us this year!" cried Marie, clapping her hands.

The children's godfather was not a handsome man. He was small and thin, with a wrinkled face and a big black patch over one eye, and he had lost all his hair, so he wore a white wig instead. But he was extremely clever. He knew all about clockwork, and could even make watches himself. If one of the fine clocks in the Stahlbaums' house ever went wrong, Godfather Drosselmeier would come and put it right. He used to take off his wig and his yellow coat and tie a blue apron around his waist, and then he would prod and poke that clock with his sharp instruments in a way which quite hurt little Marie, watching him, but which did the clock no harm. Indeed, it would start ticking and striking and chiming merrily again. And when Godfather Drosselmeier came to visit he always brought the children a present: a little doll that could make a bow and move its eyes, or a bird that popped out of a box, or something of that kind.

He always made them a very special Christmas present. What would it be this time? Fritz was hoping for a fort full of soldiers, but Marie said she'd heard Godfather Drosselmeier mention a lake in a garden, and swans swimming on the lake.

Then they tried guessing what their parents would give them. And at last, when it was quite dark, they heard the silver sound of a bell ringing. Then the doors swung open, and there stood the Christmas tree in all its glory, decorated with gold and silver apples and sugared almonds, and with hundreds of little lights twinkling like stars among its branches.

"Oh, how lovely!" cried the children, standing spellbound in the doorway.

CHRISTMAS PRESENTS

They had some wonderful presents, too. Marie was given dolls and other toys, while Fritz had a fine hobbyhorse and a squadron of hussars, very smart in red and gold uniforms. There were picture books as well, and the children were just about to look at their new books when a little bell rang again.

That meant Godfather Drosselmeier was ready to give them his present! A table stood by the wall, with a screen in front of it; the children ran over, and when the screen was taken away they saw a wonderful castle, with shining windows and golden turrets, surrounded by grass and flowers.

A chime of bells sounded, the castle doors and windows opened, and Fritz and Marie could see tiny but exquisite little ladies and gentlemen in plumed hats and long dresses, walking around the rooms. There were tiny children too, dancing to the music of the bells in the brightly lit great hall of the castle. One little gentleman in an emerald green coat kept looking out of a window and waving. And there was another, who looked like Godfather Drosselmeier himself except that he was no bigger than Father's thumb, who came to the castle door now and then, and went in again.

"Oh, Godfather, let me go into your castle!" said Fritz, but of course he was far too large. Then he wanted the little people to do all sorts of things they had not been made for, and Godfather Drosselmeier was quite cross with him. However, Mother asked him to show her how the clockwork mechanism set the little people moving, and he took it all apart and put it together again, and was soon in a good temper once more.

As for Marie, she was really more interested in the table with the other Christmas presents on it. She had seen something that no one else had noticed. When Fritz's soldiers were moved away from the Christmas tree, where they had been standing on parade, she saw a dear little man standing there as if he were patiently waiting for his own turn. He was rather an odd shape, with thin little legs too small for his body and his head, but he wore very fine clothes: a violet hussar's jacket with white braid on it, violet breeches to match, and the very best boots. His cloak was short and stiff, as if it were made of wood. Marie loved him at first sight. He had such a kind expression on his face, his large, pale green eyes were full of friendliness, and his neat white whiskers set off the sweet smile on his red mouth.

"Oh, Father," said Marie at last, "Father, who is that dear little man for?"

"Him?" said Father. "He's meant to work hard cracking nuts for both of you, my dear!" And he picked the little man up. When the wooden cloak was lifted, the little man's mouth opened wide, showing two rows of sharp, white teeth. Father told Marie to put a big nut in his mouth. Crack! The little man had cracked the shell, and Marie got the sweet kernel of the nut. "Well, Marie," said Father, "you seem to like our friend Nutcracker here a great deal, so you can look after him, though remember, Fritz has a right to use him too!" Marie picked the little man up at once and made him crack more nuts, but she chose small ones, so that he wouldn't have to open his mouth too wide.

By now Fritz was tired of playing with his new toys, so he joined Marie and laughed at the funny little Nutcracker. Then he said he wanted some nuts too. He kept Nutcracker busy, opening and shutting his mouth, and he fed him the biggest, hardest nuts he could find.

All of a sudden, there was a loud, "Crack! Crack!" and three teeth fell out of Nutcracker's mouth, leaving his lower jaw loose and wobbly.

"Oh, the poor thing!" cried Marie, snatching him away from Fritz.

"He's just silly!" said Fritz. "Calls himself a Nutcracker and can't crack nuts! Well, he's going to crack some more for me, even if he looses his top teeth too. Hand him over, Marie!"

"Oh no!" said Marie, crying. "You can't have my poor dear Nutcracker!"

"Oh yes, I can!" said Fritz. He's mine as much as yours, so give him back!"
Marie began to sob bitterly, and wrapped poor Nutcracker up in her handkerchief. The grown-ups came over to see what the matter was, and to
Marie's dismay Godfather Drosselmeier took Fritz's side. But Father said,
"I asked Marie to take special care of Nutcracker, and he certainly needs
looking after now, so we'll let her keep him. I'm surprised at you, Fritz,
expecting a man wounded in action to go on fighting! Don't you know a
good commander never sends wounded men into battle?"
Feeling rather ashamed of himself, Fritz went off to play with his hussars
again. Marie collected Nutcracker's lost teeth, took a pretty white ribbon
off her dress, and tied it around his poor chin. Then she did her very best
to make him feel comfortable, and sat nursing him like a baby while she
looked at the pretty pictures in her new book.

STRANGE SIGHTS AND SOUNDS

There was a tall, glass–fronted cupboard in the living room, where the children kept all their best toys. They could not reach up to the top shelf, which held the wonderful things Godfather Drosselmeier had made them. The next shelf down was for picture books, and Marie and Fritz could do as they liked with the bottom two shelves. Marie had made the lowest shelf of all into a house for her dolls, and Fritz quartered his soldiers on the shelf above. So now he put his new hussars away in the cupboard, and Marie moved her old doll, Miss Trudy, into a corner of the bottom shelf so as to make room for her lovely new doll, Miss Clara. Marie had some pretty doll's furniture, and a dear little bed, so Miss Clara was going to be very comfortable.

It was quite late now, and Godfather Drosselmeier had gone home, but the children could hardly bear to tear themselves away from the toy cupboard. "Come along!" said Mother. "Bedtime!"

"Oh, very well!" said Fritz. "Anyway, my soldiers need some rest too – and they'd never dare drop off to sleep while I'm around!"

So he went away, but Marie begged, "Do let me stay up a little longer, Mother! I've several things to do, but when I've done them I'll go straight to bed." Marie was a good little girl, and her kind mother knew it was safe to leave her alone with her toys, so she put out all the lights except the lamp hanging in the middle of the room, told Marie not to be too long, and went off to her own bedroom.

Marie was still nursing poor Nutcracker, and as soon as she was alone she put him down on the table, very carefully, gently untied her white ribbon, and looked at his injuries. He was very pale, but smiling in such a friendly way that it went straight to Marie's heart.

"You mustn't be cross with Fritz for hurting you, Nutcracker, dear," she whispered. "He didn't mean any harm – it's because he plays such rough games with his soldiers. But I'm going to look after you until you're quite better. And Godfather Drosselmeier will put your teeth back and straighten your shoulders!"

It was odd, but when she mentioned Godfather Drosselmeier, she thought Nutcracker looked annoyed, and his eyes flashed angrily. Marie felt quite alarmed – but next moment Nutcracker was the same as ever, and she realized it had only been the lamp flaring up that gave his face a different expression.

"What a silly girl I am!" she thought. "But I do love Nutcracker, and I must nurse him well!" So she went over to the toy cupboard, knelt down, and asked her new doll, "Miss Clara, would you let poor Nutcracker sleep in your bed? You can have the sofa. It's nice and soft!"

Miss Clara sat there looking very grand and rather peevish in her fine clothes, and did not say a word. Marie laid Nutcracker in the doll's bed, and tucked him in. Then she thought Clara looked so cross that she had better not leave Nutcracker on the same shelf, so she put the bed on the shelf above, with Fritz's soldiers, and shut the cupboard door.

She was on her way to her bedroom when she heard the faintest of rustling, scuffling sounds starting up all around her. The noises came from behind the stove and the chairs, and the other furniture. And the clock on the wall was whirring louder and louder, but it could not strike. Marie looked up and saw that the big gilded owl on top of the clock had lowered its wings to cover the face. The whirring grew louder still, and now she could make out words. "Tick, tock; clock, stop.

> Whirr so softly, hum like a top –
> the Mouse King hears, with his keen mouse ears –
> whirr, whirr, ding, dong,
> ding, dong, sing this song.
> Dong, ding, little bell ring –
> now is the time for clocks to chime."

And at last the clock struck, dong, dong, dong, twelve times, with a hoarse and muffled sound.

Marie felt scared. Then, to her alarm, she saw Godfather Drosselmeier sitting on top of the clock instead of the owl, with his yellow coat tails hanging down like wings. "Oh, what are you doing up there, Godfather?" cried Marie, near tears. "Come down! Don't frighten me so!"

But now she heard squeaking and squealing all around her, and a noise like thousands of little feet pattering about behind the skirting, while thousands of little lights came twinkling through the cracks between the floor boards. However, they were not really lights, but bright little eyes, and Marie realized there were mice everywhere, peeping out, popping out, running hippety–hop around the room. At last they drew themselves up in ranks, like Fritz's soldiers. Marie thought that was funny, and since she was not scared of mice, she had nearly forgotten her alarm when she heard a dreadful, piercing whistle that sent an icy shiver running down her spine. Right at her feet, sand and plaster and bits of brick came bursting up, and a terrible great mouse with seven heads came up through the floor. It wore seven sparkling crowns on its seven heads, and all seven mouths were hissing and squealing. Then it squeaked something to the whole mouse army, and the mice began to move, trotting on and on and up to the toy cupboard. Marie was still standing there. Terrified, she flinched back. There was a clink and a crash as the glass of the cupboard door broke; she had put her elbow through it. She felt a sharp pain in her arm – but at least the squealing and squeaking had stopped, and although she was scared to look, she thought the sound of breaking glass had sent the mice back into their holes.

But then Marie heard strange sounds in the cupboard behind her, and tiny little voices crying out, "Awake, awake, for the battle's sake! We're off to fight this very night!" And she heard the sound of little bells.

"Oh, my glockenspiel!" she cried.

She saw that there were bright lights in the cupboard, and it was full of bustle and life, with several dolls running about and waving their little arms. Suddenly Nutcracker sat up, threw off his bedclothes, and jumped out of bed, shouting, "Silly old mice, we'll get 'em in a trice! Won't that be nice? Silly old mice!" And then he drew his little sword, waved it in the air and cried out, "My loyal subjects, will you stand by me in battle?"

A number of toys, including three clowns, one Pantaloon, four chimney sweepers, two zither players and a drummer shouted out, "Yes, sir, we'll follow you to death or glory!"

Followed by the other toys, Nutcracker jumped down to the bottom shelf. It was all very well for them, since they were stuffed with cotton and sawdust, but Nutcracker's arms and legs were fragile, and he might easily have broken them jumping down. However, Miss Clara leaped up from her sofa and caught him in her arms. "Oh, Clara, how I misjudged you!" cried Marie. "You weren't cross with Nutcracker at all!"

Indeed, Miss Clara wanted Nutcracker to stay in the cupboard with her, safe from danger, but he refused. Bravely waving his sword, he jumped nimbly out and down onto the floor. And as he jumped, the squeaking and the scuffling began again. There was the great mouse army, under the big table, with the terrible, seven-headed Mouse King towering above all his men!

THE BATTLE

"Beat us a march, drummer!" called Nutcracker, and the drummer beat his drum so that the glass doors of the cupboard rattled and rang. Then the lids of all the boxes where Fritz kept his army flew open, and the toy soldiers tumbled out and jumped down to the bottom shelf too. They formed ranks, and Nutcracker marched up and down encouraging them. Turning to Pantaloon, who had gone rather pale, he said, "General, I know you are a brave commander – I put you at the head of all my cavalry and artillery. You won't need a horse, for your own legs are long enough. Do your duty!"

Pantaloon put his long, thin fingers to his lips, and let out a crowing sound like a hundred shrill little trumpets blowing. Then there was a whinnying and a stamping of hoofs inside the cupboard, and out came Fritz's cuirassiers and dragoons, and his gleaming new hussars. Regiment after regiment, they marched past Nutcracker with banners flying and bands playing, and formed up again on the floor. Fritz's cannon went rumbling out ahead of them, surrounded by the gunners, and they began to fire. Bang, bang! Marie saw them shoot sugar plums into the middle of the mice, who were soon covered with white powder. And one heavy gun battery, set up on Mother's footstool, was shooting gingerbread nuts and doing a great deal of damage.

However, the mice were still advancing, and they overran several cannon. Marie could hardly see what was happening through the smoke and dust, but both sides fought grimly. The mice brought up more troops, firing little silver balls right into the toy cupboard. Clara and Trudy were scurrying about, wringing their poor little hands. "Am I to die in the flower of my youth and beauty?" cried Clara. "Am I to perish within my own four walls?" wailed Trudy. And they fell into each other's arms, weeping so noisily that Marie could hear them even above the rest of the din – for there was a terrible noise, with the Mouse King and his army squeaking and squealing, while Nutcracker's firm voice shouted orders as he strode among his men, under fire. Pantaloon's cavalrymen had made several daring charges, but then the mouse artillery attacked Fritz's new hussars, firing nasty, smelly pellets that stained their red coats, and soon they wheeled away, leaving the battery on the footstool exposed to danger. A band of rough, ugly mice charged it so hard that the footstool toppled right over, with cannon and gunners and all. Nutcracker had to order the whole right wing of his army to retreat. However, the left wing still stood firm, although hordes of mouse cavalry had come out from under the chest of drawers to attack it. Led by two Chinese Emperors, the troops on the left advanced and formed a square. There were little toy gardeners, and Tyrolean figures, Harlequins and Cupids, lions and tigers, apes and monkeys, and they all fought well and bravely.

But then a fierce mouse captain bit the head off one of the Chinese Emperors, and the Emperor knocked several other toys down as he fell, so now the mouse army could get through the gap in their ranks. Nutcracker himself, with a small band of soldiers, was driven right back to the glass-fronted cupboard.

"Bring up reinforcements!" he cried. And some gingerbread men did come out of the cupboard, but they were poor soldiers, and the enemy soon bit their legs off.

Nutcracker was in great danger now. He wanted to scramble back into the cupboard, but his legs were too short. Inside, Clara and Trudy had fainted away, and could not help him in. His mounted men all leaped up and past him and into the cupboard. "A horse, a horse, my kingdom for a horse!" he cried desperately.

Then two enemy marksmen seized his wooden cloak. Up scurried the Mouse King, all seven throats squealing triumphantly. Marie couldn't bear it any longer. "Oh, poor Nutcracker!" she sobbed. Hardly knowing what she was doing, she took off her left shoe and threw it into the middle of the mice, aiming at their king. Then everything swam in front of her eyes, she felt an even sharper pain in her left arm, and she fell to the floor unconscious.

SICK IN BED

When Marie woke she was lying in her little bed, with the sun shining through the frost patterns on the window pane, and Dr. Wendelstern sitting by her bedside. "She's awake now," he said softly, and Mother came over and looked anxiously at her.

"Oh, Mother, have the nasty mice gone away?" whispered Marie. "Is Nutcracker all right?"

"Now Marie, you mustn't talk nonsense!" said Mother. "What's all this about mice, and your Nutcracker? Dear me, what a fright you gave us! You must have stayed up so late playing with your toys that you felt sleepy, and when something startled you – may be it was a little mouse, though we don't usually have any mice in this house – you put your arm through the glass in the cupboard door and cut yourself quite badly. I woke at midnight myself and realized you weren't in bed, so I went looking for you, and found you lying beside the toy cupboard, bleeding, with Fritz's lead soldiers and all the other toys and gingerbread men around you. Nutcracker was beside you, and your left shoe was lying on the floor a little way off."

"You see, there was a big battle between the toys and the mice," Marie explained, "and the mice were going to take poor Nutcracker prisoner, but I threw my shoe at them, and I don't know what happened after that."

Dr. Wendelstern glanced at Mother, who said very gently, "Hush dear, the mice have all gone, and Nutcracker is back in the toy cupboard, quite safe!"

Then Dr. Wendelstern took Marie's pulse again, and said she had a temperature and must stay in bed for a few days. Poor Marie was very bored. One evening Godfather Drosselmeier called to see her. "Godfather, why didn't you save Nutcracker?" she asked him, rather crossly. "You were there – why didn't you help? It's all your fault I'm sick in bed!"

But Godfather Drosselmeier was making odd faces, and humming in a strange sort of way, so that Marie stared at him, Mother herself was a

little surprised, and Fritz couldn't help laughing. "Why, Godfather, you're acting just like my old toy puppet!" he said.

"Dear me, boy!" said Godfather Drosselmeier, chuckling, "haven't you heard my watchmaker's song before?" And he sat down beside Marie and said, "You mustn't be angry with me, Marie; there was nothing I could do! But now, here's something to please you."

He put his hand in his coat, and brought out Nutcracker, with his lost teeth back in place and his jaw mended. Marie cried out with joy.

"But he's not the most handsome of fellows, you must admit," said Godfather Drosselmeier. "And if you like, I'll tell you how the Nutcracker family came to be so ugly! Have you ever heard the story of Princess Pirlipat, Mistress Mousie the witch, and the watchmaker?"

THE TALE OF THE HARD NUT

Princess Pirlipat's mother was a queen, the wife of a king, and so at the very moment of her birth, Pirlipat was a princess born. The king was delighted to have such a pretty little daughter, and he danced for joy, hopping about on one leg and shouting, "Did you ever see anything as beautiful as my Pirlipat?"

"No, never!" shouted all his Ministers, hopping about on one leg too. Indeed, there had never been a prettier baby than Princess Pirlipat. Her little face was soft and pink and white, her eyes were bright blue, and she had shining, curly golden hair. She had also been born with two rows of pearly little teeth, and she bit the Lord Chancellor's finger with them two hours after her birth, just as he was about to take a closer look at her face, thus proving to the King's delighted subjects that she was as brave as she was beautiful.

Everyone, as I was saying, was delighted except for the Queen, who seemed very uneasy, though nobody knew why. She had Pirlipat's cradle very closely watched. There were guards at the nursery door; two nurses had to sit beside the cradle, and by night there were six more nurses in the room. Each of these six nurses had to hold a cat on her lap, stroking it all the time to keep it awake and purring. You would never guess why Pirlipat's mother went to so much trouble, children, but I will tell you.

Some months before the Princess was born, a great many kings and princes came to the court of Pirlipat's father. There were tournaments and plays and balls, and they all had a very merry time. The King decided to hold a great banquet of sausages for his guests. "You know how I love sausages, my dear!" he said to the Queen. The Queen knew that meant he would like her to see to the making of the sausages herself, so she told the Lord High Treasurer to bring the silver pans and the big golden pot for boiling sausages to the kitchen. A great fire of sandalwood was lit, the Queen put on her damask apron, and soon there was a delicious smell of sausages boiling. It reached the Council Chamber, and the delighted king could not help running off to the kitchen to hug the Queen and stir the pot with his own golden scepter. Then he went back to his courtiers.

Now came the important moment when the fat bacon which was to go in the sausages must be cut up into dice and fried in the silver pans. The Queen's ladies-in-waiting stepped back, leaving this part of the work all to her. But as soon as the bacon began to sizzle, she heard a tiny voice whispering, "Give me some of that bacon, sister! I'm a queen too, and I'd like to join the feast, so give me some of that bacon, do!"

The Queen knew it was Mistress Mousie speaking. Mistress Mousie had been living in the palace for several years. She claimed to be royal herself, and said she was Queen of Mousolia, and held court under the kitchen stove. The Queen was a kind woman, so she said, "Come along, Mistress Mousie, and you may have some of my bacon."

Mistress Mousie came hopping out and jumped up on the stove, where the Queen fed her little bits of bacon as she reached out her dainty paws for them. But then Mistress Mousie's seven great, rough sons, and her

cousins, and her aunts, all came out too. They fell upon the bacon, and the Queen was so frightened she couldn't stop them. Luckily the Mistress of the Household came and chased the mice away, and there was still a little bacon left, so they summoned the Court Mathematician, and he divided it carefully between all the sausages.

Then drums played and trumpets sounded, and the King's guests all came to the great sausage banquet in their best clothes. The King welcomed them and sat down at the head of the table, with his crown on his head. They began with liver sausage, and even then the guests could see the King turn pale. He raised his eyes to heaven, and sighed pitifully, as if he had some great grief on his mind. And when the black sausages were served, he sank back in his chair, moaning and groaning and weeping and wailing, with his face buried in his hands. "Not enough bacon!" he gasped out. "Not enough bacon!"

The Queen cast herself at his feet, sobbing, "Oh, my lord, how you must be suffering! Punish me! It's all my fault... alas, Mistress Mousie and her seven sons and her cousins and her aunts ate the bacon, and..." But here the Queen toppled over backwards in a faint.

The King leaped to his feet, angrily asking the Mistress of the Household how such a thing could happen. And when she had told him the tale, he vowed to be revenged on Mistress Mousie for stealing the bacon out of his sausages.

He called in his Court Watchmaker, whose name happened to be Christian Elias Drosselmeier, just like mine. The Court Watchmaker invented several clever little machines, put a little fried bacon inside each of them, and placed them around Mistress Mousie's home. Mistress Mousie saw through Drosselmeier's tricks, but her family was not so wise. Tempted by the fragrance of that bacon, her seven sons and her cousins and her aunts fell into the traps, and were caught. Mistress Mousie went away, with only a few followers, swearing to get her vengeance.

The court rejoiced, but the Queen was anxious. She knew bold Mistress Mousie would not let the matter rest there. And sure enough, Mistress Mousie reappeared one day, while the Queen was cooking her husband's supper. "My sons and my cousins and my aunts are dead!" said she. "So take care, your Majesty – take care the Mouse Queen doesn't bite your own little princess in two!"

With these words, she disappeared again.

And that's enough for today, children! I'll go on with the story another time.

"Did you really invent mousetraps, Godfather Drosselmeier?" asked Fritz.

"What a question!" cried Mother.

But Godfather Drosselmeier smiled his strange little smile, and said, "I'm a clever watchmaker, am I not? So why wouldn't I have invented mousetraps?"

THE TALE OF THE HARD NUT, PART 2

So now, children (said Godfather Drosselmeier next day) now you know why the Queen had lovely little Princess Pirlipat so closely guarded. She was afraid Mistress Mousie would come back and carry out her threat to bite the Princess in two. The Court Astronomer and Stargazer said that only the court cat's family could keep Mistress Mousie away from the cradle. And that was why the nurses held those cats on their laps.

One night, however, at midnight, one of the nurses by the cradle woke from a deep sleep. All the other nurses were fast asleep too — and there was not a purr to be heard. It was so quiet you could hear the deathwatch beetle. And a huge, ugly mouse was standing on its hind legs with its dreadful head on the Princess's face. The nurse leaped up, with a cry of horror, the others woke too, and Mistress Mousie scuttled off into a corner of the room. The cats chased after her, but too late — she had vanished through a crack between the floorboards. All the noise woke little Pirlipat, who began wailing miserably.

"Thank goodness!" said the nurses. "She's alive!"
But when they looked at little Pirlipat, they were horrified. Her angelic
pink and white face had changed to a fat, shapeless head on a tiny,
shrivelled body. Her eyes were not blue, but green and staring, and her
little mouth stretched from ear to ear.
The Queen's grief was terrible, and the walls of the King's study had to be
padded, because he kept knocking his head against them, crying, "Oh, how
unhappy I am!" He would have done better to eat his sausages without
any bacon at all, and leave Mistress Mousie and her family in peace, but
that never occurred to him. Instead, he blamed the Court Watchmaker,
Christian Drosselmeier from Nuremberg, and he decreed that Drosselmeier
must restore the Princess to her old shape within four weeks, or at least
say how that could be done, or he would be beheaded.

Drosselmeier was much alarmed. He tried taking Princess Pirlipat apart; he unscrewed her hands and feet and examined all her insides, but unfortunately that only showed him that the bigger the Princess grew, the uglier she would become, and he had no idea what to do about it. So he put her back together and sat brooding sadly by her cradle, which he was not allowed to leave.

Wednesday of the fourth week came, and the King looked in at the nursery door, saying, "Christian Elias Drosselmeier, cure the Princess, or you die!" Drosselmeier began to weep and wail, but meanwhile the Princess was happily cracking nuts. For the first time, the Watchmaker noticed what an appetite for nuts she had, and he remembered she had been born with teeth. He asked permission to speak to the Court Astronomer, and was led to him under guard.

The two gentlemen, who were dear friends, embraced, and then they went into the Astronomer's study. Night came, and with Drosselmeier's help the Astronomer studied the stars and drew up the Princess's horoscope. At last they discovered from the horoscope that if the Princess was to be released from the spell and become beautiful again, all she had to do was eat the sweet kernel of the Crackatuck nut.

Now this nut had such a hard shell that an eighty-pounder cannon could have passed over it without cracking it. And the horoscope said it must be bitten open in front of the Princess by a man who had never shaved, and never worn boots, and he must give her the nut with his eyes shut and take seven steps backward without stumbling before he opened them again.

Drosselmeier and the Astronomer had spent three days and nights working all this out. The King was sitting down to dinner on Saturday when Drosselmeier, who was due to be beheaded first thing on Sunday morning, came rushing in, full of joy, and told him how to break the spell on Princess Pirlipat.

The King embraced Drosselmeier, promised him a diamond dagger, four medals and two Sunday coats, and said, "We'll set to work directly after dinner! Have that young man who has never shaved or worn boots ready, with the Crackatuck nut, and don't give him any wine, in case he stumbles as he steps back. He can drink all he likes afterwards!"

Stammering, Drosselmeier pointed out that he might know how to break the spell, but he had not found the nut or the young man yet, and he doubted if anyone ever would.

"Then you'll be beheaded!" roared the King furiously, swinging his scepter. However, the kind Queen begged for Drosselmeier's life, and in the end the King said that the Watchmaker and the Astronomer must both leave at once, and they must not come back without the Crackatuck nut. Then they could advertise in the papers for the young man to bite it open.

Here Godfather Drosselmeier broke off again, promising to tell the children the rest of the story next day.

THE TALE OF THE HARD NUT, PART 3

Next day, as soon as the lamps were lit, Godfather Drosselmeier came back, just as he had said he would, and went on with his story.

Well, Drosselmeier and the Astronomer had been on their travels for fifteen years without ever coming across the Crackatuck nut. Drosselmeier began to long for a sight of his native city of Nuremberg. He and the Astronomer happened to be sitting in the middle of a forest in Asia, smoking their pipes, and he told his friend how he wished he could go there.

"Well, why not?" said the Astronomer. "We might as well look for the Crackatuck nut in Nuremberg as anywhere else!"

"True," said Drosselmeier. And they both knocked out their pipes, left Asia, and went off to Nuremberg.

As soon as they arrived, Drosselmeier went to see his cousin Christopher Drosselmeier, who was a dollmaker, gilder and varnisher, and told him his story. Christopher listened with great interest, and when the tale was over he tossed his cap and wig into the air, hugged the Watchmaker, and cried, "Cousin, you're saved! Unless I am very much mistaken, I have the Crackatuck nut here!"

And he fetched a box, and took out a medium–sized, gilded nut.

"Here," said he, showing his cousin the nut, "I got this from a stranger who came to Nuremberg many years ago, offering nuts for sale. He got into a fight with the local nut sellers outside my toyshop, put down his bag of nuts to defend himself, and a heavy cart ran right over it. All the nuts were cracked but one! The stranger offered me this one unbroken nut for a shiny twenty–penny piece of the year 1720. I happened to have just such a coin in my pocket, so I bought the nut and then gilded it – I don't really know why."

The cousins called for the Astronomer, who scraped away the gilding, and found the word »Crackatuck« engraved on the nutshell in Chinese characters. The two travellers were delighted, and as they were going to bed that night, the Astronomer said, "My friend, I do believe we've found not only the Crackatuck nut, but the young man to open it too! I mean your cousin's son, and I am now about to spend the night casting his horoscope!" With these words, he tore off his nightcap, and set to work observing the stars. And sure enough, Cousin Christopher's son was a fine young man, who had never yet shaved or worn a pair of boots. He had been known as a prankster for a while, but his father had taken trouble to improve him, so that you would never know it now. He wore a fine red coat with gold braid, carried a dagger, wore a handsome wig, and had a silk hat under his arm, and he used to stand in his father's shop gallantly cracking nuts for all the young girls, so they called him Nutcracker.

Next morning, the Astronomer flung his arms around his friend and told him happily, "Yes, your nephew is the man! Now you must make him a stout wooden pigtail to work his lower jaw. But when we get back to the palace, we must wait a while before we say we've found the young man to bite the Crackatuck nut open, because I see from his horoscope that if several young men try biting the nut and fail, then the King will offer the Princess's hand to anyone who can crack it, and will make him heir to the throne."

The dollmaker had no objection to seeing his son marry Princess Pirlipat and become a prince. Drosselmeier made the young man a pigtail which turned out to work very well when they experimented on some extremely hard peach stones.

Drosselmeier and the Astronomer sent word to the palace that they had found the nut, and by the time they arrived, a number of young men, some of them princes, had assembled, trusting to their good strong teeth to break the spell on the Princess.

The travellers were horrified when they set eyes on Pirlipat again. Her tiny body, with hands and feet to match, could scarcely bear the weight of her misshapen head. And she had white whiskers, which made her even uglier.

It all turned out just as the Astronomer had foreseen. One after another, the young men tried cracking the Crackatuck nut. Their teeth and their jaws ached, and they did the Princess no good at all. As each was carried away, half fainting, to be treated by the two dentists present, he sighed, "Well, that's a hard nut to crack!"

Then the King promised his daughter and his kingdom to anyone who could crack the nut, so young Drosselmeier stepped up and asked if he could try. Princess Pirlipat liked him better than any of the others. She put her little hands on her heart and sighed, "Oh, if only he could be the one to crack the nut and marry me!"

Young Drosselmeier bowed politely to the King and Queen and then to the Princess. He took the nut from the Master of Ceremonies, put it between his teeth, pulled his pigtail – and the shell cracked open. Wiping the kernel,

he handed it to the Princess with another low bow, closed his eyes, and begun walking backward. The Princess swallowed the nut, and all at once her ugliness vanished and she stood there looking lovely as an angel, with a soft, pink and white complexion, shining blue eyes, and golden hair. Trumpets and drums sounded, and everyone rejoiced. The King and his entire court hopped about on one leg, and the Queen fainted away and had to be revived with eau de Cologne.

All this noise bothered young Drosselmeier, who still had to finish taking his seven steps backward. And as he was reaching his right foot back to take the last step, Mistress Mousie popped up through the floorboards, squealing and squeaking viciously, so that he stumbled over her and nearly fell. Immediately, the young man turned as ugly as Princess Pirlipat had been. His body shrank until it could hardly carry his big head with its staring

eyes and wide, grinning mouth. He had a wooden cloak hanging down behind to work his lower jaw, instead of his pigtail. Mistress Mousie herself lay bleeding on the floor. Her wickedness had been well punished, for young Drosselmeier had trodden on her neck. Knowing she was near death, she squealed out, "Oh, Nutcracker, if I must die, then so will you, and this is why! My seven-headed son the King will pay you back... I feel Death's sting! My life is lost – farewell, I sing! Squeak!" And she died.

Nobody had been bothering about young Drosselmeier, but now the Princess reminded the King of his promise. However, when the poor young man stepped forward, Princess Pirlipat buried her face in her hands and cried, "Oh, take that ugly Nutcracker away!" So he was thrown out. The King was furious to think he might have had a Nutcracker for a son-in-law, and banished the Watchmaker and the Astronomer from his court for ever. That had not been in the horoscope the Astronomer cast in Nuremberg, but he consulted the stars again, and said he saw that young Drosselmeier would still become a prince and a king, if he could break the spell by defeating the seven-headed Mouse King — Mistress Mousie's son born after the other seven were dead — and if he could find a lady to love him in spite of his ugliness.

So that, children, is the Tale of the Hard Nut, and now you know why people say, "That's a hard nut to crack!" and why nutcrackers are so ugly.

UNCLE AND NEPHEW

Marie had to stay in bed for almost a whole week, because whenever she tried to get up she felt quite dizzy. But at last she was better, and she could play in the living room again. When she saw Nutcracker standing in the toy cupboard smiling at her, with all his teeth back in place, it suddenly struck her that the tale her godfather had told her must be Nutcracker's own story. Yes, he was really young Drosselmeier from Nuremberg, her godfather's nephew, who had been bewitched by Mistess Mousie! For she felt quite sure that the Court Watchmaker was Godfather Drosselmeier himself. "Oh, why didn't your uncle help you?" she wailed, when she realized that the battle she saw must really have been a battle for Nutcracker's kingdom and his crown. And she told herself that Princess Pirlipat was a nasty, ungrateful girl.

At tea time that evening, Marie brought her little chair over to her godfather and sat at his feet. When there was a sudden lull in the conversation, she looked up at him and said, "Godfather dear, now I know that my Nutcracker is really your nephew from Nuremberg! And he's to be a prince and a king if he can defeat Mistress Mousie's son the terrible Mouse King in battle, so why don't you help him?"

The rest of the family laughed, all except Godfather Drosselmeier himself, who took Marie on his lap and said gently, with his strange smile, "Well, Marie dear, you are luckier than the rest of us! You're a princess born, like Pirlipat, and you rule a fine, fair kingdom. So you believe the Mouse King is persecuting poor Nutcracker? I'm afraid I can't save him myself, though. You are the only one who can do that, so you must be faithful and true!"

VICTORY

Not so long after this, one moonlit night, Marie was awakened by a strange sound in one corner of her bedroom: a pattering and a squeaking and a whistling. "The mice are back!" she cried in alarm. She wanted to wake her mother, but she could not utter a sound, or move. Then she saw the Mouse King coming through a hole in the wall. He scurried around the room, his eyes and his crowns all sparkling, and then he jumped up on Marie's bedside table, squealing, "Teehee! You must give me your sugar plums and marzipan, little girl, or I'll eat your Nutcracker up!" And he squeaked and gnashed his teeth in a terrible way before disappearing into his hole again. Marie was so scared that she looked quite pale next day. But she knew she must sacrifice her candy if she was to save Nutcracker, so that evening she put all her sugar plums and marzipan down at the bottom of the toy cupboard.

"We seem to have mice in the living room – I've no idea where they come from!" said Mother in the morning. "Oh dear, Marie, they've eaten all your candy!" And that was true, except that the greedy Mouse King did not seem to like marzipan much, so he had only nibbled at it, but it had to be thrown away. Marie didn't mind so long as Nutcracker was safe. However, that very night she heard squeaking, and there was the Mouse King again, his eyes flashing worse than ever. "You must give me your little sugar dolls," he squealed, "or I'll eat your Nutcracker up!" And off he went again.

So next day Marie went to the toy cupboard and looked at her sugar dolls. She had a wonderful collection of little people all made of sugar candy: a shepherd and shepherdess and a sheepdog, grazing a flock of white sheep; four prettily dressed couples in a big swing; a farmer and a model of Joan of Arc, and a little red–cheeked baby who was Marie's pet. Tears came into her eyes as she looked at Nutcracker. "Oh, dear Mr. Drosselmeier, I'd do anything to save you!" she said. "All the same, it's very hard!"

However, Nutcracker looked so miserable that Marie imagined the Mouse King's seven mouths opening to swallow him up, and she knew she must give up her sugar dolls too. So she put them down at the bottom of the toy cupboard, even the little red–cheeked baby.

"This really is too bad!" said her mother in the morning. "There must be a greedy mouse getting into that cupboard. It's bitten and nibbled all poor Marie's sugar dolls!"

Marie couldn't help crying a little, but she soon cheered up, and thought, "Never mind, so long as Nutcracker's safe!"

"We'll have to get a cat in, or set a trap," said Father.

"Oh, Godfather Drosselmeier can make us a trap!" cried Fritz. "After all, he invented mousetraps!"

Everybody laughed, but Godfather Drosselmeier said he certainly did have several traps at home, and he sent for one. Cook fried some bacon to put in it, and remembering the Tale of the Hard Nut, Marie begged her, "Oh, your Majesty, do watch out for Mistress Mousie and her seven sons!" And when Godfather Drosselmeier tied the bacon to a piece of string and put it in the trap, which he set beside the toy cupboard, Fritz said, "Mind the Mouse King doesn't get you, Godfather!"

However, it was poor little Marie who suffered that night. She felt something icy cold patting her arm, and something horribly rough and furry
touched her cheek, and squeaked into her ear. The Mouse King himself was
sitting on her shoulder, with his seven mouths open, all red and slobbering,
and he hissed, "Ho, ho, teehee, you can't catch me! Not with bacon, not
in a trap — I won't be caught, and that's a fact! Give me your books and
your nice new dress – give them up or you'll get no rest! And if you don't,
then you know – your Nutcracker Prince will have to go!"
Marie looked very pale and anxious next morning when Mother said,
"Dear me, we haven't caught that naughty mouse yet! But we'll soon get
rid of it. If traps don't work, we'll borrow a cat."
As soon as Marie was alone in the living room she went over to the toy
cupboard. "Oh, poor, dear Mr. Drosselmeier!" she said to Nutcracker, shedding

tears, "how can I help you now? Even if I do give the Mouse King all my picture books and my pretty new dress, he'll still want more. In the end I'll have nothing left, and maybe he'll eat me too! Oh, what am I to do?"
Suddenly she noticed a spot of blood on Nutcracker's neck. Now that she knew he was really young Mr. Drosselmeier, she didn't quite like to carry him in her arms and kiss and pet him. But she picked him up very carefully, and wiped away the blood with her handkerchief. To her amazement, she felt Nutcracker grow warm in her hand and begin to move. Quickly, she put him back on the shelf, and then his little mouth moved too, and he whispered, "Dear Miss Stahlbaum, I owe you so much! You mustn't sacrifice your picture books or your pretty dress for me – if only you can get me a sword, I'll do the rest, come what..." But at this point he stopped speaking, and the life went out of his eyes again.
Marie was not at all alarmed; she was very happy now that she knew how to save Nutcracker. However, where could she get him a sword? She decided to ask Fritz's advice, and when they were alone in the living room that evening she told him the whole story of Nutcracker and the Mouse King. Fritz thought his soldiers ought to have fought more bravely in the great battle, and told them so, but then he said, "Well, I can give Nutcracker a sword! One of my officers, an old Colonel, retired yesterday, and so he doesn't need his nice sharp sword any more!"
So Fritz brought out the retired Colonel, who was living on his pension in a corner of the shelf, and they took off his silver sword, and buckled it on Nutcracker.
Marie could not sleep that night for terror, and about midnight she thought she heard a great many strange noises in the living room. Suddenly there was a loud squeak. "The Mouse King!" cried Marie, leaping out of bed. Then all was still, but soon she heard a soft knocking at her door, and a tiny little voice saying, "Don't worry, dear Miss Stahlbaum! Good news!" Marie recognized young Mr. Drosselmeier's voice. Putting on her shawl, she opened the door, and there stood Nutcracker, with his bloodstained sword in one hand and a wax candle in the other. "Dear lady," he told Marie, "you alone gave me strength and courage to fight that wicked Mouse King! He lies dead in his own blood! Will you take these tokens of victory, from a prince who is yours until death?"
Nutcracker had the Mouse King's seven crowns over his left arm, and he took them off and handed them to Marie, who was happy to receive them. "And now, dear Miss Stahlbaum," said Nutcracker, "there are so many wonderful things I can show you if you'll just come with me! Follow me, my dear young lady – please do!"

THE KINGDOM OF SWEETS

Nutcracker led Marie to the big, old wardrobe, where she saw a pretty little cedarwood staircase coming down through the sleeve of Father's fur-lined travelling coat. They climbed this staircase, and when they reached the top, dazzling light and delicious fragrance met them. They were in Sugarcandy Meadow. They went through the Raisin and Almond Gate, into a wonderful little wood where gold and silver fruit hung from the branches, tinsel sparkled, and there was a scent of oranges all around. This was Christmas Wood. Prince Nutcracker clapped his hands, and up came shepherds and shepherdesses, huntsmen and huntswomen, all of them white and pretty as if they were made of pure sugar. The shepherds and shepherdesses performed a dance for Marie, while the huntsmen blew their horns. Then Marie and the Prince went on, beside a brook that murmured sweetly as it flowed along and smelled delicious. It was called Orange Brook.

Soon they came to Lemonade River, which flowed into Almond Milk Lake. There was another river nearby, too, with dark yellow water that flowed slowly but had a very sweet smell. Pretty children sat on its bank, fishing for fish that looked like hazelnuts, and there was a village standing beside it. All the houses were dark brown, with golden roofs.

"This is Gingerbread Village, on the Honey River," said Nutcracker. "But the people who live here are bad-tempered, because they suffer from such terrible toothache, so we won't go in."

Next they came to Barleysugar Town, where the houses were transparent, and all different colors. However, they did not stop here either; they were on their way to the capital city. And soon they reached a rose-red river. There was a scent of roses, and everything glowed in a rosy light. The light was reflected off the rose-red water, which broadened out until it was like a lake, with silver swans swimming on it. The swans wore golden collars, and they were singing the most beautiful songs, while diamond fish darted through the rosy waves as if they were dancing to the swans' music.

"Oh," cried Marie, delighted, "this is the lake with the swans that Godfather Drosselmeier was going to make me!"

But Nutcracker only laughed, and clapped his hands, and a boat came up. It was made of jewels, shaped like a shell, and drawn by two golden dolphins. Marie and Prince Nutcracker got in, and were carried over the rosy waves. As Marie looked down into the water, she saw the face of a beautiful girl looking up at her. She clapped her hands, crying, "It's Princess Pirlipat!"

"No, it's you, Marie," said Nutcracker.

Marie felt a little shy. But soon they came to land in a pretty thicket which Nutcracker said was called Sugarplum Grove. "And there ahead of us is the capital, Candy City!" he told Marie.

What a city it was, too! The houses were crowned with delicate filigree work, the towers were wreathed in leaf patterns. The city gates were built of crystallized fruits, silver soldiers presented arms as the couple walked in, and all the Prince's subjects welcomed him, hundreds of little voices shouting and laughing for joy. A great cake stood in the middle of the market place, with fountains of lemonade and other delicious drinks playing around it. Little people came thronging up: ladies and gentlemen, men and women in all sorts of national costumes, soldiers and officers, shepherds and clowns. The finest sight of all, however, was Marzipan Castle with its hundred towers, shining with lights. When they reached it, Marie heard soft music, and twelve little pages came out carrying torches made of cloves. They were followed by four beautiful ladies, who must surely be princesses. They embraced Nutcracker, and he wiped tears of joy from his eyes.

Then he introduced them to Marie as his sisters, telling them how she had saved his life. "If she hadn't thrown her shoe at just the right moment, or got me that retired Colonel's sword, I'd be dead now, bitten to death by the dreadful Mouse King!"

Sobbing, the ladies flung their arms around Marie, and they all went into a hall with walls made of sparkling crystal, full of the prettiest furniture.

The princesses set to work themselves to prepare a delicious meal, using plates and dishes of delicate china, and silver and gold pots and pans. Watching them pressing fruit, pounding spices and grating sugar, Marie wished she could help. The prettiest of Nutcracker's sisters seemed to guess her thoughts, for she handed her a little golden pestle and mortar, saying, "My dear, would you crush a little candy for me?"

So Marie happily pounded away, while Nutcracker told his sisters all about the battle... but somehow, the sounds were going farther away, veils of silvery mist were rising, there was a singing and a whirring and a humming in the air, and then it died down. And Marie herself rose on swelling waves, higher and higher she went, up and up...

THE END OF THE STORY

Bump, Marie fell from a great height. It gave her quite a shock, but when she opened her eyes she was lying in her own little bed, it was broad daylight, and there stood Mother, saying, "My goodness, how late you've slept!"

You can see what must have happened, of course: Marie had fallen asleep in the great hall of Marzipan Castle, dazed by all the wonders she had seen, and the twelve pages, or even the princesses themselves, had carried her home and put her to bed.

"Oh, Mother!" she cried. "Where do you think young Mr. Drosselmeier took me last night?" And she told her mother all about it.

"Marie dear," said Mother, when she had finished, "you've had a lovely, long dream, but you must forget it now!"

However, Marie insisted she had not been dreaming, and it had all really happened. So Mother led her to the toy cupboard, took out Nutcracker, who was standing on his shelf just as usual, and said, "You silly child, do you really believe a wooden doll can come to life?"

"Yes, Mother!" said Marie. "You see, I know Nutcracker is Godfather Drosselmeier's nephew – young Mr. Drosselmeier from Nuremberg!"

Mother burst out laughing, and so did Father and Fritz, who were in the living room. So Marie went back to her bedroom, fetched the Mouse King's seven crowns, and showed them to her mother, saying, "There! Those are the crowns the Mouse King wore, and young Mr. Drosselmeier gave them to me last night after he won the battle!"

Mother looked at the crowns in surprise. They were made of some unknown but very bright metal, and most delicately worked. Father was fascinated too, and they both wanted Marie to say where she got them. However, she could only repeat what she had said before, and when Father scolded her, and even said she was a little liar, she began to cry.

Then the door opened, and Godfather Drosselmeier came in. "Why, what's this?" said he. "My little goddaughter Marie, in tears?"

So they told him all about it – but as soon as he set eyes on the crowns, he laughed and said, "Nonsense, those are the little crowns I used to wear on my watch chain years ago. I gave them to Marie on her second birthday, don't you remember?"

Father and Mother could not remember any such a thing, but when Marie saw they were not angry with her any more she ran to her godfather. "Oh, Godfather, you know all about it!" she cried. "Do tell them my Nutcracker is really your nephew, young Mr. Drosselmeier, and he gave me the crowns!"

But Godfather Drosselmeier only frowned, and muttered, "Nonsense!"

"Now listen, Marie, you mustn't be so fanciful!" said Father, very seriously. "If you insist on saying that funny, ugly Nutcracker is your godfather's nephew I shall have to throw him out of the window, and all your other dolls too, even Miss Clara!"

Now poor Marie could not talk about her adventure any more. But she could not forget that wonderful fairy kingdom. As soon as she thought of it, she saw it all in her mind's eye, so instead of playing games she took to sitting still, thinking, and people said she was a little daydreamer.

Then, one day, Godfather Drosselmeier came to repair a clock in the Stahlbaums' house. Marie was sitting by the toy cupboard gazing at Nutcracker, deep in thought, and suddenly she burst out, "Oh, dear Mr. Drosselmeier, if you were really alive I know I wouldn't act like Princess Pirlipat, and despise you after you gave up your handsome face and figure for me!"
"Nonsense, nonsense!" said Godfather Drosselmeier.
And at that moment there was such a bang, and a jolt, that Marie fell off her chair in a faint.
When she woke up, Mother was bending over her, saying, "However did you come to fall off your chair – a big girl like you? Look, here's your godfather's nephew come from Nuremberg, so mind you're good!"
Marie looked up. Godfather Drosselmeier, in his white wig and yellow coat again, was smiling in a satisfied way, and beside him stood a young man

who was rather small but very handsome. His face was pink and white, he wore a fine red coat with gold lace, and white silk stockings and shoes; there was a pretty nosegay in his lace cravat, his hair was elegantly powdered, and he had a pigtail hanging down behind. The little dagger by his side glittered as if it were made of jewels, and he carried a silk hat.

He had excellent manners too, and he had brought Marie some beautiful presents, including sugar toys like the ones the Mouse King had eaten. And he had a wonderful sword for Fritz. At dinner, the clever young man cracked nuts for everyone, putting them in his mouth and pulling his pigtail. Marie had blushed when she first set eyes on him, and she blushed even more when he asked her to take him into the living room and show him the toy cupboard.

"Play together nicely, children!" said Godfather Drosselmeier. "All my clocks are working now, so I know you'll enjoy yourselves!"

When young Mr. Drosselmeier was alone with Marie, he went down on one knee and said, "Dear Miss Stahlbaum, you saved my life here, on this very spot. And then you were kind enough to say that you would not scorn me, like ungrateful Princess Pirlipat, if I had become ugly for your sake! As soon as you said that, I stopped being a wooden Nutcracker and returned to my own shape. Dear young lady, give me your hand, share my crown and my kingdom, and rule with me in Marzipan Castle!"

"Oh, Mr. Drosselmeier," said Marie softly, "you're so kind and good, and you rule such a lovely country, that I'll be happy to give you my hand!"

So Marie was engaged to young Mr. Drosselmeier, and after a year and a day he sent a golden carriage drawn by silver horses for her. Twenty-two thousand of the prettiest little people you ever saw, all decked in pearls and diamonds, danced at their wedding, and so far as I know, Marie and her Nutcracker Prince rule the Kingdom of Sweets to this day.

And a wonderful place it is too, if you only have eyes to see it.

E.T.A.Hoffmann was born in 1776. His Christian names were originally
Ernst Theodor Wilhelm, but he changed the third name to Amadeus as a
tribute to the composer Wolfgang Amadeus Mozart. As a young man,
he studied law, but he preferred the arts as a way of life. He could paint
and draw; he became a professional musician as composer, conductor
and music teacher; then he took to writing, first music criticism and then
fiction. Most of his stories have an element of fantasy in them, sometimes
fantasy of a frightening nature. However, THE NUTCRACKER AND
THE MOUSE KING, first published in 1819, is one of Hoffmann's
happiest tales – although even here there is something mysterious and
slightly sinister about the character of Godfather Drosselmeier, who seems
to move easily from the real to the imaginary world.
Hoffmann died in 1822 at the age of forty–six. Not only was he a musician
himself, but other musicians used his stories in their work. The ballet
COPPELIA, with music by Delibes, is based on one of Hoffmann's tales;
the same story, along with two others and the figure of Hoffmann himself,
appears in Offenbach's opera THE TALES OF HOFFMANN; and then
there is Tchaikovsky's well–known ballet THE NUTCRACKER, for which
the composer used a version of Hoffmann's story that had been adapted
into French by the novelist Alexandre Dumas.
Hoffmann's original text is over twice as long as the English version in
this book, but the translation aims to preserve the details of the plot
(which are not always quite the same as those familiar to balletgoers
from Tchaikovsky), and above all the spirit of Hoffmann the storyteller.

ANTHEA BELL